George L. Reid

The Heather Bell

And Other Poems

George L. Reid

The Heather Bell
And Other Poems

ISBN/EAN: 9783743417168

Manufactured in Europe, USA, Canada, Australia, Japa

Cover: Foto ©Andreas Hilbeck / pixelio.de

Manufactured and distributed by brebook publishing software
(www.brebook.com)

George L. Reid

The Heather Bell

THE

HEATHER BELL

AND

Other Poems,

BY

GEORGE L. REID,

MENASHA, WIS.

1891.

THE

HEATHER BELL

—AND—

Other Poems,

GEORGE L. REID.

MENASHA, WIS.

1891.

THE HEATHER BELL.

The blushing rose is beautiful,
 The lily fair to see,
The daisy with its lowly head
 Blooms on the grassy lea:
The yellow primrose ever fair
 Adorns each shady dell;
But fain I rather would behold,
 The purple heather bell.

The fragrant clover decks our meads
 In clusters bright and red,
The cowslip too, can there be seen,
 With dew its lips are fed.
And oft the sweet forget-me-nots
 Of love their story tell;
But best of all I love to see
 The purple heather bell.

The lovely flowers our gardens yield
 Are beautiful and fair,
Their gorgeous hues and lovely tints
 Are features rich and rare.
I gaze on them with pleasure deep,
 My heart with rapture swells,
But yet I love amid their bloom
 The purple heather bells.

The bees from flower to flower will fly
 In search of honey dew
And many a time in vain they try
 Those flowers of gorgeous hue:
But set them down in August time
 On moor and heathy fell,
Of honey sweet they sip their fill
 From purple heather bell.

I've wandered oft in summer time
    By rippling burns and rills,
I've climbed with strong and steady limbs
    My native heather hills ;
I've laid me down and musing there
    On tales of foreign fell,
I vowed I never would forget
    The purple heather bell.

And now in this far distant land
    With plenty ever blest,
The land of love and liberty,
    The land of peace and rest,
I muse on all the by-gone years ;
    My mem'ry weaves a spell
Around the joys of boyhood's days
    And purple heather bell.

THE AULD MAN'S RECOLLECTIONS.

In the land o' my birth to me dearest on earth,
    In the land o' auld Scotland, far ower the deep sea,
I mind weel lang syne when this young heart o' mine
    Was stown by a lassie, sae pawkie and slee.
I lang, lang did woo her and said I did lo'e her,
    That for her dear sake I was maist like to dee,
Till her heart I did move wi' the sweet words o' love
    And gat her consent my ain dear wife to be.

Then when married fu' fain in a house o' oor ain,
    We baith were as cosie as bodies could be ;
When seated sae snug by the auld chimla lug,
    We would crack wi' ilk ither, my wifie and me.
And when wee bairnies came to oor dear winsome hame,
    They lichtened oor hearts wi' their innocent glee,
Sae blythe and sae blate, I worked air and late,
    And we baith were sae happy, my wifie and me.

But awa ane by ane frae oor side they were ta'en,
    By the fell hand o' Death, a grim tyrant is he !
And for mony a day in dool sorrow and wae,
    We lamented their ganging, my wifie and me.

Though much death bereft us, yet ane still is left us,
  To cheer our old age by the licht o' his e'e ;
He is kind to his mither, we are dear to ilk ither
  My own dawtie boy, my wifie and me.
Noo auld age creeps o'er us and death is before us,
  But me and my wifie we dread na to dee ;
Our wark is maist dune and the Faither abune
  Will sune steek the een o' my wifie and me.
We cease noo oor moaning as comes on life's gloamin',
  For sune our dear bairns we again hope to see,
And meet them forever across the cauld river,
  To dwell a' thegither in mansions sae hie.

CENTENNIAL POEM ON THOMAS CAMPBELL.

A hundred years have passed away
  Across the dial stone of time,
  O'er Scotia's stern and rugged clime,
Since Thomas Campbell's natal day.

To-day, a hundred years ago
  This greatly gifted man was born ;
  No peal of bells nor trumpet horn
Proclaimed his birth to friend or foe.

Born in Albin's commercial mart,
  Where flowers bloomed on the banks of Clyde :
  And sweeping out upon its tide
Sailed freighted ships for every part

Of earth's dominions : every clime
  They visited with wealth and goods
  From field and mine and storied woods,
At morning's dawn or evening's chime.

Well pleased his mother saw the fire
  Of genius sparkling in his eyes,
  While adding to the many ties
That bound her to his worthy sire.

In youth, while feeble in his frame,
  He wandered often by the side
  Of Cora Linn or Falls of Clyde
In search of health, the vital flame.

At school his genius brightly shone,
  For often in the classic race
  With soaring wings and swifter pace
The goal he reached, the prize he won.

Well purified and well refined
  By varied learning, rich and rare,
  And art's fine treasures garnered there
His youthful cultivated mind.

With prescient eye his fancy saw
  Himself the Rector's place secure
  In after life with heart as pure
As when he walked the Broomielaw.

He saw the last of human kind
  Address the glowing orb of day
  And bid it hasten on its way
To fell destruction sure destined.

While he with his immortal soul
  Of all things yet should see the last
  Depart and fade into the past
Ere he should reach the heavenly goal.

With sympathy his bosom burned
  For Poland's cause, for Poland's weal,
  And active his unflagging zeal
That Russia's power should be o'erturned.

That Poland evermore be free,
  Was his own dear intense desire,
  And brightly burned that patriot fire ;
But woe, alas! it could not be.

Scotland, my dear, my native land,
  From Thee hath sprung a numerous host
  Of noble names, our pride and boast,
To adorn and grace thy sea-washed strand.

TRIBUTE OF THANKS

TO EMILY CHARLES HAWTHORNE, FOR POEM ON BURNS.

Respected Madam, now this line
I send to thee for favor fine,
Which thou didst grant to me and mine
    On Burn's night ;
By far the best of poems thine,
    And full of light.

I'm glad thou dost appreciate
The writings of our bard so great,
Who is (though born of low estate)
    The king of song ;
But who so early met his fate
    And stayed not long

To clink the words and make them jingle
By grassy howe or heartsome ingle,
And deign with honest folks to mingle
    At kirk or fair,
And with an eye forever single
    To praise them there.

We thank thee for thy poem fine,
For every verse, for every line,
The which with wit and sense did shine
    High over all
Who did upon the muses nine
    Attempt to call.

Thy praise of Burns is well deserved,
Yet still thy power may be reserved,
Thy heart and pen the more be nerved
    To sing his fame,
Who from his duty never swerved
    Nor his great aim.

With manly independent heart
He nobly used the poets art
To aim and shoot the pointed dart
    At fraud or guile,
While men of sense with wit alert
    Did laugh or smile

To see how he exposed their cant,
Their rhodomontade and their rant
About religion : showed their want
      Of real true grace
Who still with hypocritic vaunt
      Lengthened their face.

Thy "flower of verse from freedom's shrine
Of him who sang of auld lang syne,"
We'll cherish aye, line upon line,
      While life shall last.
We pray God's blessings on thee and thine
      May now fall fast.

And when thy life's last vital thread
Shall snap in twain, and thy fair head
Shall pillowed be among the dead
      In church-yard low,
May friends around thy narrow bed
      Express their woe

By thy sweet and pure reflection
As pictured in their recollection,
Thy every good and worthy action
      While in this life,
And thy constant true affection
      As maid or wife.

Adieu, Dear Madam, and this rhyme
Excuse on part of me and mine,
Our thankfulness inspired the line
      We send to thee.
May favors from on high be thine,
      Now and for aye.

POEM

COMMEMORATING THE 80TH BIRTHDAY OF ABRAHAM
LINCOLN.

Though humble his birth and low his estate,
Though rough his young life and hard was his fate,
He did triumph o'er all of the ills of life,
And came out the victor at last from the strife.

Though hard were his labors in life's early youth,
Yet strong his young heart and valiant for truth.
He did climb by hard paths to the fair heights of Fame,
And engrave on those heights an immortal name.

Through many reverses he rose up at last
A hero to conquer over every rude blast
That beat on his bosom so loyal and true.
No deed of his life had he e'er cause to rue.

To the highest position his country could give,
He attained by his wisdom and prudence to live
For her weal and her good through her darkest hour,
And nobly he wielded his God given power.

When treason arose and with wild ruthless hand
Essayed to destroy our fair fertile land.
Espying the danger he grappled with might
To subdue the monster and uphold the right.

And when had appeared the fulness of time
He did rise in grandeur to height sublime ;
With the words of his pen, by a hand true and brave
He did strike off the fetters from every slave.

He sent to perdition that cursed institution
That sullied the page of our fair constitution,
No more to disfigure, no more to deface,
A whole nation of freemen we now take our place.

Ever true through the nation's dreariest hour,
He did wield with wisdom his wonderful power
To redeem her highly dear honored name,
And place her o'er all on the bright scroll of fame.

But his country's enemies, maddened and pained
By the conquest that truth and right had obtained,
With one cruel blow laid him bleeding alone
To seal with his blood the great work he had done.

Then his country bewailed the sad loss of her chief,
And his martyr death plunged her deep into grief,
And his countrymen followed with woe deep and sincere
To his last resting place his pall and his bier.

Remembering his worth and remembering his fame
We praise and admire his much honored name ;
We would pass down that name in traditional story
Enshrined as it is in a halo of glory.

Ye comrades once in arms, Oh! forget not the woe
Which our country in these her dark hours passed
   through,
And the peace which your valor and prowess attained
Transmit to your sons e'er unsullied, unstained!

ANNIVERSARY POEM ON BURNS.

READ AT RYAN'S HALL, INDIANAPOLIS, JAN. 25, 1877.

We meet this night to celebrate the birth
 Of Burns, whose fame extended wide
As soul and king of song o'er all the earth ;
 We point to him with grateful pride.

And while o'er all the world, in every land,
 They meet to honor him whose song
Binds heart to heart, joins hand in hand,
 And brothers make of every gathered throng.

We too, his countrymen, assembled here
 With joy around this festive board,
Will hail again the birthday with good cheer
 Of Scotia's son, the ploughman bard.

In a lowly cot on the banks of Doon
 Was Burns, the peasant poet, born ;
No pomp attended on the birth of one
 Whose songs are sung at eve and morn.

In early youth auld Scotia's genius fair
 His steps pursued while at the plow,
While warbling birds in feathery plumage rare
 Sang sweet on every branch and bough.

And viewing oft his manly form and face,
 With haste she near and nearer drew,
Till o'er that form with matchless queenly grace
 Her mantle she divinely threw.

Saying, "Hail king of poesy and song,
 To thee this mantle I bequeath,
Attune the harp which long hath been unstrung,
 Sing sweetly o'er thy native heath."
Then lowly kneeling at her feet
 The youth with grateful homage bows,
And modestly in tender accents sweet
 With honest fervent heart he vows
To sing dear Albin's hills and fertile vales,
 Her rivers clear, her lakes and woods,
Her mountain steeps sublime, her flow'ry vales,
 Her light cascades, her roaring floods,
Her maidens blythe and fair, her honest men.
 In glorious verse and fitting rhyme
He finished this great task, laid down his pen
 And died while yet in early manhood's prime.
And now let us this night resume
 His praise who sang so sweet, so well,
And who like yonder silvery shining moon
 Doth o'er us cast a magic spell.
All hail to Burns, the king of song and mirth,
 The soul and joy of minstrelsy,
Destined though but a peasant at his birth
 To reign in human hearts for aye.
Dear Caledonia, though far from thy shore,
 We dwell on Columbia's fair strand,
We'll cherish thy glorious memories evermore,
 Our own, our dear, our native land.

THE YOUNG WIFE'S SOLILOQUY, OR MY WILLIE AND ME.

In the days o' lang syne when a lassie sae wee
Aye careless and lightsome, as happy's a bee,
I roamed ower the heath or spield the green braes
Free as a bird a' the lang simmer days,
And cam' hame at e'enin' doon laden wi' flowers
Culled by wee hands frae nature's fair bowers ;

Oh ! they were as bonnie as bonnie could be,
I tauld my dear minnie wi' joy in my e'e.

A' simmer a bare-fitted lassie I roved
Through the fields and the lanes I sae lang dearly loved,
Awa over the knows or deep doon in the dells,
Gatherin' the bonnie braw Scottish blue bells,
Or the wild bits o' gowans that grew on the lea
To mak' into posies for mither and me;
I thought na o' walth and I kent na o' fame
But was well satisfied when at e'en I cam' hame.

And when winter would come and cauld winds would
      blaw
And cover the earth wi' a mantle o' snaw,
Fu' cosie inside we would sit round the fire
And list to auld tales we did sae much admire.
"As bonny Kilmeny ga'ed down the long glen
Where fairies did dwell and where nae ane did ken,
O what happened to her when she was awa
But she cam' back no the same being ava."

Sae the lang winter nights passed cheerily by,
Tho' loud blew the winds and black was the sky,
And for mony a year the time passed awa'
Till at last I the time of young womanhood saw,
When wi' laughin' and daffin I gaed mony a gate,
And sune I was brought face to face with my fate,
For strappin' and tall and fu' gracefu' was he
And warmed my heart wi' the kind look o' his e'e.

Oh ! he aye sought me oot and wi' me he would gang
To market or fair and ne'er think the road lang,
O' a' the folk that I saw it seemed unto me
That nane were mair happy than Willie and me,
Till at length for his coming I impatient did wait
In the lang simmer e'en doon by the yard gate,
And then his "good e'enin'" would make my heart dirl
And set a' my bosom and head in a whirl.

Time swiftly sped by as we wandered together,
We were seldom apart though stormy the weather,

When he spiered for my hand wi' a smile on his face
I gied him my promise wi' a good heart o' grace.
Sae sune we were married, tis some years since gane,
And I ne'er rued the day when my heart it was ta'en,
But I bless aye the day that we met wi' ilk ither
And thus far in true love we live happy together.

Sune there cam' to oor home a wee bairnie fair
Wi' bloom in her cheeks and bonnie fair hair,
Which made us mair closer to ilk other move
An added link o' affection to bind us in love,
Fu' fondly we welcomed this wee bond sae dear,
And we plighted oor faith that this being sae fair
Would hae oor peculiar fond parental care.

Then to better oor state my dear Willie did sail
For the land o' the west, and blest was the gale
That wafted him ower the wide stormy main
And brought back the news of his safety again.
When two years had sped the guid kindly chiel,
Wha in the meantime had done unco weell,
Did send for us baith whom he much wished to see,
And we were reunited, my Willie, the bairn and me.

There a cosy wee home for us a' he had made
In a bonnie wee hoose underneath the saft shade
O' the maples sae green that stood by in the street
Where flowers also shed forth their odor sae sweet.
Noo twa years hae sped in this far-awa' land
And anither ane is added unto oor bit band,
Sae we creep aye the closer and fu' kindly agree
To lo'e ilk ither mair fondly, my Willie and me.

O lang may it be sae and lang, lang may we lo'e
Ilk ither wi' hearts ever faithfu' and true,
In constant affection while life shall endure
May our lives like a stream grow mair and mair pure,
Sae that when at the last oor bit race here is run
And the last battle ended, the last victory won,
Having safely glided over this life's fitful sea,
May we land safe in heaven, my Willie and me.

POEM

WRITTEN FOR THE TWENTY-SEVENTH ANNIVERSARY OF
THE BIRTH OF ENOCH PERRY, MENASHA,
MARCH, 1890.

Swift changing time speeds on apace,
   Year after year rolls o'er each head,
Marking new lineaments in the face
   Till all is done and we are dead.

Those young in years would fain they sped
   More swiftly till to manhood grown,
Thinking they drag by a lengthened chain
   A heavy load to the vast unknown.

While the old think winged pinions broad
   Bear them along with rapid flight
As if they were but a trifling load ;
   To them they seem but as a night.

And so the birthdays come and go,
   To some glad steps in the path of life,
To others only bringing sad scenes of woe
   And burdens heavy and ceaseless strife.

His birthday here, what are the joys
   That fill his heart with a glad refrain ?
Is he satisfied with the gaudy toys
   Of this fleeting world, those trifles vain ?

No, I wot not; his thoughts arise
   To things sublime where glory shines,
To the pastures green of fair paradise
   Where he revels while writing those gracious lines

That come from his lips in promise sweet
   To the faithful ones soothing their fears,
How they together in glory shall meet
   After the flight of life's few short years,

In a happier clime where sorrows ne'er come
   To dim the eyes or sadden the heart,
For the Light of that world shall be the Lamb,
   And all shall share a glorious part.

We come, dear Brother, with words of cheer
  On this return of thy natal day,
Rejoicing with thee that another year
  Of safety and joy has passed away.

That yet you are spared your mission to fill,
  With prospects fair of the years to come,
That with added zeal you may press on still
  With greater speed to your heavenly home,

May God in his love give you strength and health
  To proclaim his message of love to all
Who hear your voice : for what is wealth
  Or this world's gain if we hear not the call.

Our Father, we pray thou wilt bless this home,
  The father and mother and children dear,
With peace and joy in days to come,
  And happier still be each passing year.

May one and all here so run the race
  In the heavenly way to the land of rest
That they may behold thy dear smiling face,
  With their Saviour dwell forever blest.

POEM.

OOR AULD FRIEND JOHN.

I ha'e wandered muckle through this weary warl,
  I ha'e met wi' queer men noo dead and gone,
But in mony respects I ha'e ne'er seen a carle
  Sae funny and queer as oor auld friend John.

I ken fu' weel he canna sing a sang,
  O' music within him there's never a tone,
But weel pleased he will listen the haile night lang
  To ither folk singing, oor auld friend John.

But few sic men as oor friend can be found,
  Wi' like lear in their heads, as we must own,
Ye will no aften find them the warld around,
  Sae wise and sae learned as oor auld friend John.

He can quote you extracts o' verse or prose
　　Frae writers that lang ha'e been dead and gone,
As Burns, Scott, Byron, Hogg, Campbell and those
　　O' many mair countries, oor auld friend John.

O' ups and downs he has had his ain share,
　　And dool sorrow and woe as time has flown
Has saddened the heart and whitened the hair
　　O' this guid kind fallow, oor auld friend John.

Yet bravely he has borne the rude world's shock
　　'Gainst his peace and his life, well nigh overthrown,
But stands after a' as firm as a rock
　　In the midst o' a tempest, our auld friend John.

Noo this wee bit o' rhyme I maun draw to a close,
　　Though his virtues I trow are no half shown,
That he has mony mair ilka ane here knows
　　He is a douce guidman, oor auld friend John.

When we meet together sae blythe and slee
　　Wi' quib cracks and jokes that are a' his own,
He will draw oot the fun with mirth and glee
　　Frae the lave of the chields, oor auld friend John.

Aye when we forgather to drive awa care,
　　We raise oor pavilion and set up oor throne,
And then we select ane the night's croon to wear,
　　Wha d'ye think is the king but oor auld friend John?

Sae here's his guid health and lang may he live
　　To rule this great people around him that's grown,
The best in his realm to them may he give,
　　And kind be the rule o' oor guid King John.

TRIBUTE OF WELCOME TO JOHN S. REID,

RECTOR OF SAINT PAUL'S CATHEDRAL, INDIANAPOLIS,

AFTER HIS RETURN FROM VACATION SEPT. 1, 1878.

Though thy absence from us hath been brief,
We have missed thee much, our worthy chief;
Thy presence in our midst once again
Is like bright sunshine after rain.

We welcome thee back to our throng
With smiles, by voice in speech and song,
For thee our hearts are filled with love,
To thee with outstretched hands we move.

A happy people greet you here,
Their Pastor, Friend and Brother dear,
These smiling faces round thee tell
The love which in their hearts doth dwell.

Now while we spend a happy night,
While every eye beams clear and bright,
While joy abounds in every heart
May each, may all act well their part

To welcome thee as each sees best
To loving labors after rest.
Those labors may the Master bless
And crown them ever with success.

May heaven's choicest blessings now
Descend and rest upon thy brow,
May peace and plenty e'er be yours
While hope and life and time endures.

And when thy labours here are o'er,
When men shall see thy face no more,
May angels guide thy spirit home
High up to Heaven's ethereal dome.

A ROMANCE OF REAL LIFE.

The sun was sinking in the West
   Ower bonny fair Dundee,
The sangsters o' the deep wild wood
   Were mute on ilka tree,
The shadows o' the e'ein' time
   Were gathering thick and fast,
A' sounds o' joyous life were hushed
   Declaring day was past.
Sweet was the witching gloaming hour
   And tranquil was the scene

Where twa young lovers fondly met,
  By a' the world unseen,
To take a sad and lang fareweel,
  For he was gaun to see
If fortune in a distant land
  Would be mair kind and free.

"Sweet lassie," said the loving lad,
  "My heart is only thine,
And when I shall be far awa
  Let not your heart repine;
For I'll be aye, aye true to thee
  Where'er I distant roam,
And soon should fortune smile on me
  I'll make for thee a home,
And I will send for you, my dear,
  It's peace with me to share,
Then through the future o' life's years
  We'll part no nevermair."

"Oh! laddie dear, I'm wae to think
  We soon shall parted be,
But swear by all the powers abune
  To faithful prove to thee,
And patiently whate'er betide
  I'll await the message fair
That bids me hasten to thy side
  Thy joys or griefs to share.
Sae when you're far frae me awa
  O dinna e'er forget
Your plighted troth to keep heart true
  And never for me fret."

The hours sped on while this fond pair
  Plighted their vows to keep
Whate'er should happen them while apart,
  Divided by waters deep;
Little mair did they say for thought
  Was busy within each mind,
She dreaded the parting soon to come,
  He sighed to leave her behind.

At last the farewell words they spake,
  The tears stood in their e'en,
He hied him off with a heavy heart,
  She grat when a' unseen.

Out on the ocean sailing fast
  A brave ship held her way,
Each bending spar and straining mast
  Told the breeze held well its sway,
And her human freight with ardent hope --
  Were musing while on she bore
Them all through the white and billowy foam
  To a far off fertile shore.

On that vessel's deck our young hero stood,
  His thoughts went back to the night
When he parted from her in the deep greenwood,
  While the tears came and dimmed his sight,
Yet hope rose in his heart as he gazed o'er the sea,
  And whispered of plenty in the land of the West,
How fortune would smile on his labors and toils,
  When success should attend and he should be blest,
So proudly all his fears to the breezes he flung
  And cheerily, merrily thus now he sung:

"Roll on, deep blue sea, in power and might
And bear our good ship until land comes in sight,
On hope's pinions borne I'll toil not in vain,
But succeed in my mission across the deep main."

The voyage now ended, o'er the deep waters blue
To eager eyes watching the land comes in view,
Very soon the staunch vessel reaches the shore
And lands now in safety all those whom she bore ;
Our hero now landed he flies to the West,
For there he had thought his chances were best,
And by rail at last reaching far Winnepeg,
But there for employment in vain did he beg ;
Discouraged, disheartened, he starts for the states
Where a full home of plenty his coming awaits.
Soon swiftly the message is borne o'er the sea,
"Come now, my lassie, Oh ! come unto me,

Here cosy beneath the maple's green shade
A home of contentment for thee I have made.''

The message received, she quickly prepares
To share now with him his joys or his cares,
Her friends and relations she bids an adieu
And sails off with joy o'er the deep waters blue ;
The vessel speeds on in her course o'er the main,
The two hearts will soon be united again.

The land soon appears o'er the watery brim
And seems a fair haven as it did unto him,
She lands and soon safely then borne on the rail
She meets him and thus nears the end of our tale,
For soon after this the banns are proclaimed,
The time is appointed, the day it is named,
And this night these two lovers you've seen made one.
My story is ended, my task it is done.

DAY BY DAY.

A pilgrim in a stranger's land
  With weary steps my feet doth stray,
Oh ! let me hold thee by the hand
  And guide me safely day by day.

Swift years roll round the course of time
  And the moments quickly speed away,
Oh ! lead me now while in my prime
  And guide me safely day by day.

Should clouds and storms e'er gathering fast
  Obscure by gloom the narrow way
Lead me till storms and clouds are past
  And guide me safely day by day.

Should sin and satan tempt my life
  And fill my soul with bleak dismay.
Give strength, Oh ! aid me in the strife
  And bring me safely through the fray.

When health shall fail and limbs grow weak,
　When this poor body shall decay,
Then kindly Lord unto me speak
　And guide me safely all the way.

When life's short fitful fever's o'er,
　When longs my soul to flee away,
Then Saviour guide me to that shore
　Where beams the bright eternal day.

THE DARKEST HOUR IS JUST BEFORE DAWN.

If at times through this life our hearts e'er grow weary,
　And in sorrow oft sighing we bitterly moan,
Let us ever remember though all seems so dreary
　The hour that is darkest is just before dawn.

If the lean hand of poverty grasp at our life,
　And with hunger's keen pangs we oft inwardly groan,
Let us still muster courage and renew the strife,
　The hour that is darkest is just before dawn.

If those who in time of prosperity were friends,
　Should in days of adversity leave us alone,
Let us still battle on to accomplish our ends,
　The hour that is darkest is just before dawn.

If some sick friend appears to be nearing the tomb,
　Who lately in health sported o'er the green lawn,
Let us still cherish hope he'll be spared to our home,
　The hour that is darkest is just before dawn.

OUT ON THE LAKE.

Out on the lake on a summer day fair,
Breathing the fresh invigorating air,
Out on its waters with a joyful crowd
Where laughter and mirth are frequent and loud,
Sailing along o'er the deep swelling waves,
E'en when the storm and the mighty wind raves,
When nature with life is alert, awake,
Oh ! it is grand to be out on the Lake.

Out on the Lake, like a deep mirror wide
Where the white winged boats so rapidly glide,
You can see them reflected within the clear waves
While around and about them the water laves ;
The gull on its broad wings is sweeping along,
While we hear in the distance the fisherman's song,
Much health and content from its bosom we take,
Oh ! it is pleasant away out on the Lake.

Out on the Lake keenly watching the race,
We see eagerness painted on every face,
As bounding away from the start they go
Like an arrow shot from a very strong bow.
See the yachts stretch away before a brisk gale,
While about and behind them many a sail
Is following forth in their glassy wake
Intently watching the race on the Lake.

Out on the Lake, we are now bound for home,
Our good ship cleaving the billowy foam,
While far to each side the land can be seen
Clothed in dense foliage of living green.
Speeding on swiftly all hearts are gay
As bathed in the light of declining day
With joy of pleasure our fill we partake,
Oh ! it is fine to be out on the Lake

WRITTEN FOR THE 120TH ANNIVERSARY OF THE BIRTH
OF ROBERT BURNS, 1879.

We meet this nicht to celebrate
The birth o' nae great potentate,
But peasant bard sae blythe and blate,
  Dear Bobbie Burns,
Wha lang has gane the weary gate
  We gang by turns.

Noo sax score years ha'e fled awa'
Since he his breath began to draw,
Whan winter winds aroond did blaw
  Sae keen and cauld,

And filled the doors wi' driving snaw,
     Auld Boreas bauld.

The kin folks round wi' anxious care
Did view his face sae young and fair
But little kenned what kind o' ware
     There was comin',
Until the gossip versed in lear
     Unco woman

Did ower him bend wi' winsome smile,
To tell his fortune she did toil
Whilst ithers waited a' the while
     To hear his fate.
Hoo he should sing ower Scotia's isle,
     And be na blate.

To sing whate'er should please himsell,
To sing what unto him befell,
To sing by burn and woody dell
     The lassies braw
That he did woo and lo'e sae well
     By birk or shaw.

To sing o' nature's honest men
In cantie but or cosie ben,
The chields that he sae well did ken
     And lo'ed to meet,
And wha deserved the praise his pen
     Laid at their feet.

To sing "Ye banks and braes of Doon"
And "I'll gang nae mair to yon toon"
Or the "Bonnie Mary Morrison
     As lichts a fairy
And that sae sweet to bonny tune,
     His Highland Mary."

To sing o' "Tam O'Shanter's mare,"
To sing aboot "The Holy Fair,"
"First when Maggie was my care"
     Or "Duncan Gray,"
"O' wandering by the banks o' Ayr
     Ae winter's day."

To sing o' "Nancy, Nannie, Jean,"
And ither lassies too I ween,
He met by leafy shaw or green
    When he was young.
In praise o' maist braw lassies seen
    His harp he strung.

Wi' manly independent breast
Richt bauldly he himself exprest
Before the rich, though he their guest,
    When questions rose,
And Lords did think that they kenned best
    Ower Athole brose.

And wha while lords and ladies fine
Aft ower a glass o' rosy wine
Would make him a' his friendship tine,
    Plied a' their art,
Yet minded aye the days langsyne
    And kept his heart.

While passing up auld Reckie's Street
Wi' gentleman sae sleek and neat,
An honest friend he chanced to meet
    And to him spak,
As glad his old time friend to greet
    As though his back

Was clad in best o' guid braid claith
That was wae waur for wear or skaith,
As though braw and warm it was baith,
    As e'er could be ;
He met him wi' as muckle faith
    And hearty glee.

When he reached again the lordie's side,
The cuif a' wrapped up in his pride
Did daur the honest bard to chide
    In haughty strain.
Tauld him his fame there wadna bide
    If e'er again

He spake to sic' like lookin' men
The rich nae mair the bard would ken,
And he should quit just there and then
    And na mair to them chat.
Bauldly he said wi' tongue and pen
    "A man's a man for a' that."

For friends to him were friends indeed,
Though toilers for their daily bread,
Though farmers plowing ower the mead
    Wi' dinna care ;
Wi' blessings he bade them God speed
    To muckle mair.

For Robie was a clever chiel
Wha ne'er ta foe did shaw his heel
And feared nobody ; e'en the de'il
    He dared address,
As he wi' sturdy step did spiel
    Up Parnassus.

Let us rejoice again this nicht
In Burns, oor bright and shining licht,
And ne'er through life of him lose sicht,
    Nor a' he's dune,
Till we in regions clear and bricht
    Meet him abune.

THE WOODS.

How pleasant to be in the woods
In the balmy month of June,
Where upon the high tree tops
Each bird is singing a tune,
A hymn of praise to the Creator above
For His bountiful mercy, His wonderful love.

How beautiful are the groves,
How grateful is their shade,
When from the heat of the scorching sun
We seek the forest glade
And silently there in the solitude
We recline at our ease in the leafy wood.

How fragrant the summer air
With the perfume of new mown hay,
How beautiful, glossy and fair
Are the birds in their plumage gay
As they flit about on the wanton wing
And joyously, merrily, happily sing.

How cool and refreshing the breeze
Unto the sufferer's cheek
As under the shade of the trees
He health for his body doth seek.
It raises his spirits, brightens his eye
And he thankfully raises his voice to the sky

Saying, "Father, I offer my heart unto Thee
And thank Thee for all of Thy kindness to me,
For succor received from Thy bountiful hand
When the wheels of this life were nigh at a stand,
For all of the blessings Thou hast bestowed
When burdened with cares like a heavy load,
When I almost despaired of life and of hope,
And constantly fretfully ever did mope,
Although from the hands of benevolent love
Rich blessings were showered daily on me from above,"

ODD FELLOW'S MOTTO.

FRIENDSHIP, LOVE AND TRUTH.

Friendship is the true bond of life
  That shall with each succeeding year
Dispense all fratricidal strife
  And quench for aye distrust and fear.
Then war shall cease throughont the earth
  And peace shall reign serenely bright,
And plenty take the place of dearth
  Where all was gloom and brooding night.

Love then shall shed a golden beam
  Upon each home and family,
Or like a silvery gliding stream
  From heart to heart flow swiftly.

Then happy, all with one accord
   Shall thankful stoop and bow the knee
To heaven's high majestic Lord,
   Our King through all eternity.

Truth shall prevail o'er all the land
   And Error foul shall be laid low,
Then all men, Brothers of one band
   Their friendship, love and truth will show
In deeds of mercy to the poor
   Who need their aid and sympathy,
And every house with open door
   Shall entertain the stranger free.

IN MEMORIAM.

ON THE DEATH OF MATTHEW PERRY, INDIANAPOLIS.

But yesterday to us he seemed
   So hale and hearty for this life,
So strong and able as we deemed
   To battle in this rough world's strife.

But alas ! for human expectation
   Of what the future forth will bring,
Without one short day's intimation
   He felt the power of death's rude sting.

Snatched suddenly from our little band
   His face no more our eyes shall see,
No more will press his loving hand
   Nor feel the thrilling ecstacy.

Of joy and friendship warm our hearts
   As round and round song follows song
At our reunions : for death's darts
   Have silent made our brother's tongue.

Genial and kind with us he mingled
   Greeting us with a friendly smile,
Each one amongst us aye he singled
   To shake our hand and chat awhile.

Inquiring kindly for our welfare
  Or how we prospered by the way,
Happy to hear if we did share
  A taste of joy from day to day.

And if the world's sorrows touched us
  Plunging us deep into woe and grief;
His sympathizing words e'er reached us,
  His hand afforded prompt relief.

We'll miss him, aye we'll miss him sadly
  When round again comes Burn's day,
Where he would have been right gladly
  To pass the merry hours away.

We sorrow with his bereaved friends,
  His daughter, son and loving wife,
Hoping when their race on this earth ends
  They shall meet him in a bettter life

Where cares and sorrows ne'er shall come,
  Where partings shall forever cease,
Where in a bright eternal home
  The good shall dwell in perfect peace.

IN MEMORIAM,

ON THE DEATH OF ALEXANDER MATHEWSON, INDIAN-
APOLIS.

A short time ago he came to our city,
  A lonely young man, lowly humble and poor,
Homeless and friendless enlisting our pity,
  And in want he called at our workshop door.

He left his own land far away o'er the sea
  To seek for wealth on Columbia's shore,
He left his relations with heart light and free,
  Little recking that they should see him no more.

But soon these fond hopes he cherished were blighted,
  The fair golden dream from his fancy had fled,
When here in this city sad and benighted
  Our aid he desired to procure work and bread.

He little expected to starve in a land
  Where plenty was said to exist evermore,
And where far away from his loved native land
  All enough might receive of the new world's store.

With our assistance he procured work at last,
  His immediate wants very soon were relieved,
Hope returned to his heart so lately down cast
  And freely amongst us life's pure air he breathed.

With high aims and bright prospects his bosom now
      burned
  Since winter had fled with its mantle of snow
Ahd glowing with beauty bright spring had returned
  Driving far from his bosom the feelings of woe.

His life for some time then he seemed to enjoy,
  A pleasant companion with heart light and free,
Of life's pleasures drinking though mixed with alloy,
  His countrymen often desiring to see.

But alas !, ah ! too soon disease with its pain
  Laid hold on his vitals, encompassed his life,
Hope fled from his heart on its plumed wings again
  And Death soon released him from sorrow and strife.

We followed the bier with his corpse to the grave,
  His remains in the dust we laid down with care,
While around that sad spot the willows did wave
  We fervently breathed for his mother a prayer.

Oh ! may he who tempers the wind to the lamb
  Prepare her fond heart for the news of his death,
Who though far away was her own darling son
  And murmured her name with his last dying breath.

Soothe her, Oh ! Lord, with thy comforting spirit
  For the loss of her son so far, far away,
And may they together dear heaven inherit
  And dwell there united the long endless day.

EPISTLE

TO MY BROTHER AND SISTER, JOSEPH AND MARY
PICKARD, NEAR LEEDS, YORKSHIRE, ENG-
LAND, FEB. 1886.

While winter with his icy hand
With mighty grasp enfolds the land
   And holds it fast secure,
While winds around my dwelling blow
And deeply lies the glistening snow
   So beautiful and pure,
I sit me down to pen this line
   To thee so far away
Who should be dear to me and mine
   While life holds still her sway,
   With good will I hope still
   To merit thy esteem,
   So stay for and pray for
   A new poetic gleam.

Remembering the days langsyne
When but a lad I saw thee fine
   So stalwart and so tall,
So vigorous in brain and limb,
So full of life, so full of vim
   Thou stood the peer of all,
A sturdy oak of English birth
   Thou wert in days of yore,
And firmly trod thy mother earth
   When little past thy score
   Of life's years without fears
   Such was near thy age,
   Thy young life 'gan the strife
   Of battle fierce to wage.

Across the wild Atlantic main
Thy welcome letter safely came
   And cheered my grateful heart.
With joy my inmost bosom burned
As o'er and o'er I deftly turned
   Its pages on my part,

And read the message there revealed
  Of kindred love and joy,
Which from thy bosom now revealed
  Were lavished on the boy
  Who on a time in Scotia's clime
  Dwelt with thee when a child
  And found there thy tenderest care
  His infant hours beguiled.

Though many years since then have fled
And passed o'er that once childish head
  His heart is still the same,
Tender as when in youthful glee
He lovingly prattled on thy knee
  And sought thy love to claim.
Though wandering far from thee away
  He strives yet for the right,
That he may meet thee on that day
  There in that land of light
Where ever seen with joy supreme
  We behold our Savior dear,
Where not a sigh will e'er come nigh
  To cause a single tear,

And my dear sister, thy dear wife,
I mind what joy in early life
  I often had with her,
Who eldest of the children was
Yet never proved herself the cause
  Of making any suffer,
But rather by her kindly aid
  Did help us on our way
When bairns trials sair dismayed
  In that our life's young day.
She cheered oft and cleared oft
  The thorny paths we trod,
She bade us and made us
  Bear up beneath our load.

Thy letter duly came to hand
From thy far and distant land,

The home of Britons true,
Who for a thousand years or more
Did wage their wars upon that shore
  Against a tyrant crew,
Till they at last the victory gained
  O'er tyrany and might.
And freedom to the world obtained
  By conquering in the right.
Ne'er fail then to hail then,
  These noble Britons bold,
Those freemen, those strong men
  Who lived in days of old.

Oh ! God, our friend and father dear,
Who se'est us shed the bitter tear
  For many a wayward sin,
Forgive us, Oh ! forgive, we cry
And help us with thy grace to try
  To conquer and to win
The victory of every foe
  That doth assail us here
And seeks to bring eternal woe
  And doom our souls to fear.
Thou who art love, enthroned above,
  Who for us bled and died,
Be near anon and cheer us on.
  E'er keep us by Thy side.

And now my brother and sister too
I bid you for awhile adieu,
  And kindly to you send
Our warmest love and true affection,
As shown by this our first exertion
  In rhyming to a friend.
I hope to have your answer soon
  To this bit screed o' mine,
And trust before the next new moon
  You will indite your line.
No more the muse we will abuse
  By driving her too fast,
But let her rest when at her best
  That she may longer last.

EPISTLE

TO JOHN WILKINSON, INDIANAPOLIS.

Noo auld freend John, I take my pen
To write a line to you agen
   Wham I lo'e weel and dear,
In answer to your kindly letter,
I trow I couldna get a better
   Frae ony far or near.
It cheered my heart to read it ower
   And a' the news you sent
To praise ower weel is yout my power
   But I am weel content
   Sae thinkin' I'm clinkin'
   Some thochts into a rhyme
   That ye may see what I could dae
   Had I but just the time.

Your letter found me unco weel
And it werna for the muckle deil
   Wha aye is trouble raisin'
By using his satanic arts
Upon our poor, weak, sinfu' hearts
   Oor fralities ay praisin'.
He'd make us think oorsells sae guid
   That we ha'e naught to fear.
As if we werna flesh and bluid
   And didna shed a tear
Ower mony sins and shortcomin's
   That vex us real and sair
And mak' us sigh as we draw nigh
   To God in earnest prayer.

Ootside the wintry blast is blawin'
And light snaw flakes are quickly fa'in
   Doon on oor mither earth,
While cosie by the warm fireside
Fu' snug I sit and safe abide
   Sae favored frae my birth,
Wi'a the blessings o' the years
That noo are past and gane,
Though I had mony griefs and fears

And muckle toil and pain,
Hoo gracious and precious
　My heritage has been
Showered on me, poured on me,
　Frae Loves ain hand unseen.

Your letter lies before me noo,
A welcome visitor I trow
　As e'er I've had of late,
Wi' a' the news that it contains ;
I thank you kindly for your pains
　But lang for it did wait.
I'm glad to ken ye've been sae thrang
　Wi' needle and wi' shears
Fitting the bodies o' the gang
　I hope for joy—no tears,
Auld prick the louse I hope ye're crouse
　And canty a' at hame.
Noo bear wi' me and hear frae me
　I speak na to your shame.

Noo dinna tak' it sair to heart
Ye were sae lang to tak' a start
　To answer scrap o' mine ;
Time mak's a' things richt they say,
And brought your letter safe a'e day
　Around my heart to twine.
The words o' love o' former years
　When af'times we would meet,
Those kindly words a't brought the tears
　Those messengers sae sweet
Overflowing, thus showing
　The heart's love deep sincere,
Caressing and blessing
　We hailed ilk ither dear.

"For human frailty alas,"
These are your words I would impress ;
　To err indeed is human,
But I would add to this your line
That to forgive is sure divine,
　Greater than virtue Roman

Wha boasted o' heroic deeds
   On fields of battle gory
But never had it in their creeds
   To forgive the greater glory.
Then imitate and cultivate
   This gift indeed o' grace,
That beaming and gleaming
   It may shine in thy face.

Sae —— —— and his guid wife
Ha'e lately been enjoying life
   By traveling abroad,
A crossing ower the deep wide sea
Seeing o' Lunnon and Paris
   And making their abode
In many a distant far off clime,
   Seeing Cockneys and their ways, .
Or ower the channel for a time
   Sayin' "parlez vous francaise,"
Or hearin' them swearin'
   "Eh, bien, Sacre Dieu "
Wi' wonder to wander
   And then at last adieu.

And —— —— oor guid auld freen,
Ye surely mony sights ha'e seen
   Sae lang ye've been awa',
I vow I'd like to have been wi' ye
And place after place had seen wi' ye
   And gi'en them a' a ca'.
Can ye no write and gi'e a description
   O' places that you've seen
And speak your mind without restriction
   As ye should to a freen?
Reveal then and heal then
   My curiosity,
Inditing thee, inviting thee,
   I ask it o' your pity.

But —— —— takes the cake
In simmer at Minnetonka Lake
   Where rich folks gang a fishin'.

Then in the winter at New Orleaus
As if he were a man o' means
   Guid luck to him I'm wishin',
Though it would seem his lot is fickle
   As ever fell to ony,
But I trust for a' he has a pickle
   O' the ready money
To freely use and na abuse
   Whate'er he has to spare,
When meetin' wi' and greetin' wi'
   His auld freens guid and rare.

I suppose when Burns' day cam' roun'
In your bit inland railroad toon
   Ye were made unco happy,
Gathering together fra'e laud o' Scots
And o' ane anither takin' notes,
   I doubt na ower the nappy
Which durin' the night ye'd aften sip
   As freen after freen did greet ye
While frae the heart borne on the lip
   Were words o' love, aiblins o' pity.
Sons o' heather met together
   Are a happy sight to see,
Sae freendly greetin' ilke ither meetin'
   On that night frae care set free.

Noo fare ye weel the muse must rest
I trow wi' me she's dune her best,
   I here frae her maun light
And dinna wi' my lines be hard ;
Ye ken I'm but a lowly bard
   Yet striving to be right.
And answer soon wi' heart o' grace
   This limpin' cripple rhyme,
For I would like to see your face
   And hope to yet sometime.
Noo fare ye weel and bear ye weel
   The burden o' your years
And think o' me when this ye see
   Wi' a' my griefs and fears.

EPISTLE,

TO JAMES MCLAREN, NEWARK, NEW JERSEY.

Some thirty years have passed awa'
Wi' simmer sun and winter snaw,
Since in your toon sae far awa'
    I first ye kent.
When to the grove we hied us a'
    On pleasure bent.

I mind fu' weel the place sae fine
Where wi' the compass and the line,
Either it was wi' tape or twine,
    We made the rinks
When you and Sandy McGregor syne
    Played sic high jinks.

Ye pitched the quoits and made them whirl
Fast through the air wi' sic' a swirl,
And finely ye did mak' them birl
    Doon on the pin ;
Aft 'gainst ilk ither they would dirl
    Wi' siccan din.

Ye chose me to your play direct,
I did dae sae wi' great respect,
I aften had to sair reflect
    Hoo ye should play ;
My duty I did na neglect
    Upon that day.

While Sandy's man, big buirdly chiel.
Was fu' o' fun and ettled weel,
He fu' o' confidence did feel
    Aboot his man,
And aften turning on his heel
    He would us bann.

But jist fu' pawkie and fu' slee
A word or twa or hint I'd gi'e
When a' sae neat upon the tee
    Your quoit gaed smack ;
I tauld them then wi' muckle glee
    To gi'es their crack.

And sae the game went slowly on,
Ye got a shot and then anon
He'd get anither as oft upon
    The pin he lay.
Ower siccan play the sun ne'er shone
    As on that day.

But time was ca'ed before the game;
Mair than half dune it was a shame,
But weel ye tried to make ye're fame
    Ring near and far;
Noo at this day nane can ye name
    But as a star.

Well, Jamie lad, nae doot ye mind
The lad wha left you far behind
A'e April day ye were sae kind,
    To see him go
Borne on the wings o' steam and wind
    For weal or woe?

His native land received him sound
Withouten either hurt or wound,
And his folks a' weel he found
    Glad him to greet,
But noo a' laid by in the mound
    Beneath oor feet.

I was sorry to see you hurt yoursel',
Ye must ha'e slipped and nearly fell,
Just how 'twas dune ye couldna tell,
    Twas dune sae quick,
But this ye ken ye're back sae well,
    Has noo a crick.

But noo I ken ye're wonderin', thinkin
Wha this bit o' rhyme is clinkin',
While thochts aboot your brain are jinkin'
    Without remead.
It's only I wi' sleep near blinkin',
    George Lindsay Reid.

EPISTLE,

TO MY BROTHER, JOHN L. REID, DANVILLE, ILLINOIS.

My ain, my kind and only brither,
Besides you noo' I ha'e no ither,
And what to say I'm in a swither,
  For my neglect
I should be licket ower the wither
  Into respect.

A year has nearly come and gane
Since ye wrote me kindly and fu' fain,
But proscrastination is my bane,
  In writing letters;
I should be burdened wi' a chain
  Or bound in fetters.

But noo frae hence I vow and swear
Gin ye wi' me will langer bear
Sheet after sheet to write and tear
  Till I shall please ye,
Your mind and body baith to wear,
  Guid faith I'll tease ye.

Your letter cam' the ither day
And made my heart baith blythe and gay,
For mair success I yet would pray
  In time to come,
And that guid luck wi' you might stay
  And a' your home.

I read your letter ower and ower
And glad was I 'twas in your power
To rise abune the cloud and shower
  O' fortune's blast,
Till ye your millions three or four
  Should sune lay past.

Then live in auld age at your ease
Wi' nocht to vex but a' to please,
Having plenty o' this world's 'crease
  To oil life's loom
Till it wear oot and ever cease
  In silent doom.

Though puir mysel' I still am canty
And aften I am prood and vauntie,
Saying to myself let naething daunt me
    O' wordly care,
As long's ye're weel and aye have plenty
    O' hamely fare.

I'm sittin' by the fireside thinkin'
These thochts I into rhyme am clinkin'
Sometimes they flee and after jinkin'
    Aboot awhile,
I catch them up as they are sinkin'
    To durance vile.

But noo I maun draw to a close
Or else frae verse drap into prose ;
But for this time this mcde I chose
    O' ryhmin' news,
The truth to you I will disclose
    Forced by the muse.

My wife and I send a' oor love
To you and your's though far we rove,
May peace e'er like a brooding dove
    Sit in your hame,
And mercy point the way above
    A shining flame.

THE LUNCH STAND.

—— —— ——, he keeps a lunch stand neat
At the corner of Illinois and Washington Street,
And there you can get of everything plenty
From a fine selection both rare and dainty,
    Right tiddy faloo, faloo, fala ra day,
    Right faloo ral a—

As you walk down that way his place you'l espy
And if you are hungry don't pass it by,
But step inside and your order in a trice
Will be served up to you both rare and nice.

There he has pork and beans and pickled pig's feet,
And ham and eggs so fine to eat,
Or steak and potatoes—a very fine dish,
And should you prefer, you can have some fish.

Or should you want oysters just wait a short while,
He will serve them up to you in any style,
Either raw or fried or scalloped too—
Or better, you can have a splendid stew.

No——he is a very fine fellow,
Polite and friendly and very mellow,
Begotten I assure you of a very fine stock,
He can enjoy with any a very good joke.

Then take my advice and give him a call
If anything you should want to eat at all,
He will do what is right by you every time
If its only to the small amount of a dime.

A PRAYER.

Weak and sinful though I be,
    I approach Thee, gracious Lord
And ask that Thou would'st unto me
    Some promise of Thy word afford;
Some precious blessing let me find
    That I may honor Thee still more,
Pure make my humble contrite mind
    And I will praise thee and adore.

Save me henceforth from all the sin
    Which hereunto in my life has been
A thorn to rankle in my breast.
    Wash Thou and make me ever clean ;
Oh! glorify thyself in me
    Thou maker of all things below;
Oh! may the thoughts that dwell in Christ
    Into and from my mind e'er flow.

To those with whom I have to deal
    May some kind word and thought be given
Which may into their bosom steal
    And turn their thoughts from earth to heaven ;

So thus may I from day to day
   Become more useful, Lord, to Thee,
That when my life has passed away
   I may enjoy eternity.

"Come angels ever bright and fair,"
   Thy loving watch o'er us to keep,
Near hover in the midnight air
   And guard our persons while we sleep.

With brighter hopes our life renew,
   Stay close beside us all the while,
Our hearts keep ever pure and true,
   Prevent our lips from speaking guile.

At early morning when we wake
   Prompt us to sing sweet hymns of praise
To Him who dwells above the skies,
   To Him of everlasting days.

Angels watch ever o'er our home,
   Thy loving vigils o'er us keep—
Unto our side at twilight come,
   Oh! guard us ever while we sleep.

IN MEMORIAM

TO MY DEPARTED WIFE.

Oh ! where art thou Beckie, the joy of my hear
Oh ! why my dear darling so soon did we pa
In Elysian fields dost thou ever more roam?
Oh ! where, tell me where, is thy bright spirit home?
Thou beautiful being so dear unto me,
Oh ! when shall my eyes thy fair spirit e'er see,
When join thee amongst the bright spirits above
And breathe in thy ear the sweet accents of love?

I think of thee, Beckie, by night and by day,
And longs my sad spirit to hasten away
To regions of bliss where thy spirit so fair
Doth breathe in the fragrance of perfumes so rare.

Then watch for me, Beckie, for soon I will come
And welcome me, darling, to heaven, thy home,
There ever to dwell in those regions of light
Where bright day ever smiles unclouded by night.

THE RIVER SAINT JOE,

Let great poets sing of their fair flowing rivers
   Meandering through lovely valleys so green,
Where the beam of the sun on their clear water quivers
   And lights up with beauty each dear sylvan scene.
Where all is delightful and pleasant and sunny,
   Where flowers of great beauty in profusion grow,
I will sing of a river the equal of any
   It is no less a stream than the river St. Joe.

Its lofty green banks gaily decked with bright flowers
   Are truly reflected within its clear stream,
There are many enchanting and natural bowers
   Where lovers may wander and poets may dream,
Where swift by these bowers with a gay rippling motion,
   E'er glistening and sparkling its pure waters flow,
No river deserves more a poet's devotion
   Than this swift flowing stream, the river St. Joe.

Flow on thou fair river and sing while thou'rt flowing,
   As oft thou hast done in the days long ago,
E'er the red man beheld thy waves warmly glowing
   Or dashed o'er those waves in pursuit of his foe.
Flow on in thy beauty by hills and through meadows
   Where the crops of the husbandman flourish and grow,
Here kissed by the sunshine, there hid by the shadows,
   To thy rest in the lake, thou lovely Saint Joe.

COLLECTION OF HYMNS.

Oh! Jesus, source of every joy
   That fills each humble Christian heart,
Those pleasures are without alloy
   Which thou to thine dost e'er impart.

Oh ! what delightful hours are those
  We spend before thy throne in prayer,
When to Thy side we each draw close
  Any see Thee fairest of the fair.

By faith we see thee on the cross
  For us Thou died upon the tree,
For us Thou counted all things loss
  That Thou from sin might set us free.
And now our hearts to Thee would cling,
  Our eyes behold our pardon there,
Now all we have to thee we bring
  Oh ! Thou the fairest of the fair.

And when at last we come to die
  Cease struggling for a parting breath,
Wilt Thou then waft our souls on high
  And help us conquer in our death ?
Wilt thou receive us in that clime
  To greet our friends already there
And join with them in praise sublime
  Of Thee, the fairest of the fair ?

HYMN.

Above all joys we can possess
  While here on earth below,
Above all joys that truly bless
  Which human hearts can know,
There is a joy o'er all supreme
  Which soothes the troubled breast,
'Tis found beneath the mercy seat
  Of all our joys the best.

It is the sense of pardoning grace
  Which fills the heart with peace,
'Tis found by faith, retained by faith,
  It never more shall cease,
But surely grow while here below,
  A bud of promise given
To bloom at last when life is past
  A lovely flower in heaven.

I would that all this joy may find,
  So precious to the soul,
Its peace will satisfy the mind
  While endless ages roll,
In heaven above redeeming love
  Will e'er our tongues employ,
To sing the glorious glad refrain
  Will be our dearest joy.

Then may we tune our voices here
  To praise the Saviour's name,
And cry aloud the joyful news:
  Behold! Behold! the Lamb
Who once was slain upon the tree
  That sinners he might save,
But lives again to ever reign
  Victorious o'er the grave.

LIFE FOR A LOOK.

Look away to Jesus, weary soul,
While sin's billows round thee rudely roll,
  Though the tempest rages high
  In a stormy cloud tossed sky,
  He will see thy pleading eye,
      Weary soul.

'Tis written in the book, weary soul,
There is life for a look, weary soul,
  He will send thee joy and peace
  And from sin thy soul release,
  To thy heart for e'er give ease,
      Weary soul.

Then thou shalt sing for joy, happy soul,
Praise shall e'er thy lips employ, happy soul,
  Christ shall ever be thy song
  As to heaven you move along
  Soon to join the blood washed throng,
      Happy soul.

With grateful hearts may we resolve
  To do the Master's will
And while the years around revolve
  The post of duty fill.

May praise attend upon our lips,
  In our hearts dwell love divine,
May future work the past eclipse
  And each lamp brighter shine.

The Lord shall be to us a tower
  Of strength in time of need,
His grace shall give us greater power
  To do each noble deed.

Let us take each other by the hand
  And vow e'er to be true,
And nobly an unbroken band
  Be bold to dare and do.

HYMN.

Master, another week has sped,
Another Sabbath day has fled,
And e'er to rest I lay my head
  I ask what have I done for Thee.

Something from Thee I've tried to seek,
Some words for Thee I've tried to speak,
And though I have been very weak
  I've done some work I trust for Thee.

I worshiped Thee among the throng
And felt thy presence us among,
I sang Thy praise in sweetest song,
  So much, dear Lord, I've done for Thee.

And now before I seek my rest
I ask for what Thou seest best,
That I may be most truly blest
  With strength to do more work for Thee.

HYMN.

I heard a voice from Calvary's mountain
  Say, weary sinner come to me,
Drink from me the living fountain
  And no more e'er thirsty be.
Thy sins have all been laid upon me,
  I will wash their stains away
If only you will hearken to me
  And in the future watch and pray.

That voice I heard and went to Jesus
  And drank of that life-giving stream,
He came to me who from sin frees us
  And changed the spirit of my dream ;
So now the glory of his presence
  Is my joy by night and day,
While praying that his kindly guidance
  May keep me in the narrow way.

SABBATH BELLS.

Those Sabbath bells how sweet they ring
To cheer our hearts and make us sing,
Of heavenly joy their music tells,
I love to hear those Sabbath bells.

Those Sabbath bells, their cheering voice
 Bids every sin-sick soul rejoice,
Tell Jesus died on Calvary,
Tell how God loved humanity.

Those Sabbath bells they call along
To praise and prayer and sacred song,
They call to worship true, sincere
In this sweet spring time of the year.

Those Sabbath bells, their joyous peal
Soothes every care, and make us feel
Our sins forgiven through Christ the Lord
Because we trust him and his word.

PATRIOTIC SONGS.

The banner of our country fair
  Is o'er us streaming fairly
And as it floats out on the air
  Its stars are beaming clearly.
    That flag of old, each fold on fold,
    Let all true men from hill and plain,
    From shore to shore our country o'er
Vow still to love more dearly.

Ye hardy sons of rustic toil,
  Revere the emblem which you see,
Let no slave live upon the soil
  Your fathers fought and bled to free.
    Then swear for e'er that flag to bear
    In serried ranks, in strong phalanx,
    Whene'er a foe shall strike a blow
Against your lives or liberty.

This glorious land of your's and mine
  Is freedom's shrine and altar.
Then guided by the hand divine
  Press on and never falter,
    Sing freedom's song, its notes prolong
    Till o'er the sea all men are free,
    And with like praise their voices raise
To heaven for freedom's shelter.

TUNE, "AMERICA."

Our country, ever dear,
Where all from far and near
  May dwell in peace ;
Here ever clear and bright
Shines freedom's holy light
To greet our grateful sight
  And never cease.

Blest country of the West,
Of all the lands the best
  Under the sun.

Let us preserve her name
High on the scroll of Fame,
Long burn the sacred flame
    Our sires begun.

Great God ! with grateful praise,
Our voices we would raise
    To Thee in song,
For blessings which thy love
Sends daily from above,
May we e'er thankful prove
    A happy throng.

TEMPERANCE POEMS AND SONGS.

ANNIVERSARY POEM OF MENASHA LODGE 85, I. O. G. T.,
OCTOBER 19, 1889.

TUNE, "What the Bells Said."

The leaves were red and yellow,
    The autumn sun shone bright,
All nature sear and mellow
    Was pleasing to the sight ;
The birds still hovered round us
    And trilled their notes forth sweet,
The grass and sweet leaved clover
    Lay crisp beneath our feet,
Sending fragrance forth on the warm balmy air,
    Happy birdies singing, singing ;
I then thought to myself, all the world is blest
    And we are joyously marching on.

With words of earnest import
    Our Grand Chief came along,
He stirred our minds to action,
    Our lips to ardent song ;
He told the baneful story
    Of Rum's accursed sway,
And how in pain and anguish
    Full many a victim lay,

How 'twas sweeping them downwards to drunkards'
        graves,
    Swiftly, sadly, surely, madly,
Of many broken hearts who in deep sorrow mourn
    And wearily wend life's way.

    He urged us on to action
      Beneath our banner fair,
    To stem the tide of evil,
      Nor give up in despair ;
    We heard his urgent pleading,
      We joined the temperance band
    Now marching on to conquest
      Throughout our native land ;
As we go we sing now with heart light and free,
    Glad songs, gay songs, sweet songs, brave songs ;
For the future is bright with fair hopes we see,
    As we steadily march along.

    One year has now since sped onward,
      And the battle we've bravely fought
    By gathering into a safe fold
      Many lost ones whom we have sought.
    So now with numbers strengthened
      We wage the war still on,
    Enkindled with fresh courage
      By the victories we have won ;
Still with earnest hearts and with purpose true,
    Gravely, stoutly, bravely, boldly,
We will step to the tune of the temperance song
    And so fearlessly march along.

TOUCH NOT THE WINE.

Let those who may drink of the fruit of the vine
And sip with delight of the rosy wine
As it sparkles and shines so bright and so fair—
It is a deceiver, a demon lurks there.
Ah ! fatal to them will the draught be at last,
When the mirth and the joy are faded and past,
For down to the deepest of depths will they go
And suffer the doom of an endless woe.

Then touch not the wine
Though it sparkle and shine,
Be it Moselle or Rhine
It will bite like a serpent at last,
And sting like an adder when pleasure is past.

Many in youth have become its vile slaves
And deeply disgraced have filled drunkard's graves,
Who might have attained all of life's great ends
And proved a great blessing to family and friends ;
But they drank of the wine and it maddened their brain,
They drank of the wine and it blasted their name,
They drank and it led into folly and crime,
Whose lives might have been made forever sublime.

CHORUS :

Now let one and all here exercise self restraint,
And avoid with deep loathing the slightest attaint
Of the venom that lurks in its death-dealing bite,
Whose end is dark death in oblivious night ;
Then dash down the cup full of rosy wine,
Nor e'er again raise it to lips of thine,
But ever engage against it in strife
And drink, only drink, the pure water of life.

CHORUS :

TUNE, "Todlin hame."

While here a' alane I sit and I think
Hoo aft wi' the lads I ha'e ta'en a drap drink
To pass awa' time or drive awa' care,
But noo I am dune and will bumper nae mair,
    Bumper nae mair, bumper nae mair,
But noo I am dune and will bumper nae mair.

I thought to mysel' I ha'e tippled ower lang
And sae to tell a' I write this bit sang,
O' this world's troubles we a' ha'e oor share
Without the drap drink that brings mony mair;
    Bumper nae mair, bumper nae mair,
Sae come noo my friends and bumper nae mair.

Oh ! leeze me on drink, its a harmfu' thing,
Aud aye leaves 'ahint, a sharp, sair sting,
To injure oorselves is indeed na fair
Sae let us break aff and bumper nae mair;
    Bumper nae mair, bumper nae mair,
Sae let us break aff and bumper nae mair.

There's mony a man that would fain gi'e ower
But drink has got him sae much in his power,
Made him to his friends a burden o' care,
Glad would they be did he bumper nae mair,
    Bumper nae mair, bumper nae mair,
Glad would they be did he bumper nae mair.

Come tak' my advice and fu' happy you'll be,
As blythe as a lark and as busy's a bee,
The haill day lang you will sing evermair
And prood you will be that you bumper nae mair,
    Bumper nae mair, bumper nae mair,
And prood you will be that you bumper nae mair.

SONGS.

OH ! JOHNNY COME BACK AGAIN.

For sometime past I must confess
  My heart's been sad and full of woe,
And oft I've thought 'twas not amiss
  That I should wish to see my beau,
And when he came here to see me to-day
  His face appeared so bright and cheery
That my spirits were raised up right away
  And my heart at once grew gay and merry.

CHORUS :
    O Johnny come back again, my dear,
      I beg you don't stay so long away,
    For I must confess when you are here,
      My heart is happy, light and gay.

The birds sing sweeter on the trees,
  More beautiful doth bloom the flowers,
With fragrance laden seems the breeze
  And swifter fly the winged hours ;

The world more joyous doth appear,
  I am happy all the livelong day
When beside me is my own dear,
  He drives each sorrow and care away.

CHORUS:

Now I and he are going to marry,
  Oh! soon I hope to call him mine,
Till that day comes I scarce can tarry
  My heart with his fore'er to twine;
Oh! happy then my heart shall be
  With Johnny ever by my side,
My husband he, so dear to me,
  And I his joyous, loving bride.

CHORUS:

SONG.

He wooed and won my trusting heart
  When I was beautiful and young;
For well he plied the lover's art
  With his fond looks and flattering tongue;
He praised my shapely comely form,
  He said my face was fair to see.
And from life's bitter pelting storm
  Oft promised he would shelter me.

I loved him better than my life,
  I worshipped him almost I trow,
And through the future care and strife
  Would have soothed his throbbing fevered brow,
I yielded to his fond embrace,
  With him life's sweetest joys did share,
But with a heart devoid of grace
  For me and my love did he care.

SONG.

While far from thee, dear native land
  Now sad with weary feet I wander,
And think of thy fair sea-washed strand
  Where lingering memory loves to ponder;

Thou land where oft in childhood's hours
  My feet have pressed thy blooming heather
And quaffed in thy enchanted bowers
  Sweet pleasures gone alas forever.

By Devon's winding crystal stream,
  With youthful careless footsteps straying
I've watched beneath the sun's clear beam
  Its waters glistening, rippling, playing ;
There in the pleasant summer time
  While flowers on its banks were blooming
I've heard the distant church bells chime,
  Their sounds my lips to praise attuning.

Oh ! Scotia, land of heath and broom,
  Land of the torrent lake and fountain,
Where bright blue bells in beauty bloom
  Upon each hill and towering mountain.
Now while in this far distant land
  I read of thee in Scottish story,
And think of all thy heroes grand,
  I'll love thee for thine ancient glory.

SERENADE.

Dear lady fair, awake, Oh ! awake from thy slumbers,
While far across the lake the breeze wafts my sweet num-
    bers,
My harp's sweet tuneful string sounds to the loving strain
Which for thine ears I sing as I seek thy bower again.

The moon shines bright and clear in the heaven's deep
    azure blue,
And sheds her silvery light over everything I view.
While quiet reigns around come listen to my song ;
With love life's pulses bound I would not detain thee long.

Oh ! wake my lady fair, but if an enchanting dream
As light and thin as air, like a gentle murmuring stream,
Still binds thy senses fast in slumbers soft and deep
My strain will soon be past, then no more my watch I'll
    keep.

Farewell, young lady bright, now ends my melodious lay,
For e'er the morning light I must hie me far away,
But I'll remember thee though in distant lands I roam,
And soon as I am free I will seek thy mountain home.

SONG.

I lo'ed a lass wi' raven hair,
    She was a lovely lass I ween,
She was sae tender, true and rare,
    And had twa bright black sparkling een ;
She met me wi' a winsome smile
    Whene'er I gaed the lass to see,
And wi' a heart aye free frae guile
    I aft her sweet red lips did pree.

When simmer days were lang and warm,
    Wi' ither lasses aft I've been,
But nane my heart could ever charm
    Like this dear lass, my bonny Jean.
Noo through the future o' life's years
    Until the very day I dee
Amid my joys, my griefs and fears,
    My bonnie Jean, I'll mind o' thee.

SONG.

We are a' frae the land o' the thistle and heather,
    We are a' frae the land o' the brave and the free,
And while here the night we forgather together
    May we spend it sae canty wi' wit, mirth and glee.

Oor forefathers fought bravely ower mony a field,
    Oft defeating the Norman, the Saxon and Dane,
Swiftly driving them back with the claymore and shield
    Over mountain and vale to the shore of the main.

When the English invaded our dear native land,
    Then bold Wallace the banner of freedom unfurled   }
And led into battle his brave warlike band,
    Till back from their hamlets the tyrants they hurled.

Then now let us sing her brave sons and fair daughters
  Wha still live to add to her glory and fame,
And though far far across the wide waste of waters
  May we lo'e and aye cherish that ever dear name.

Then here's to the land o' the thistle and heather,
  The land o' a people sae brave and sae free,
And joyfully aft let us forgather together,
  Although her blest shore we may nevermore see,

ADDED VERSE TO A SONG ENTITLED, "HER BRIGHT
SMILE HAUNTS ME STILL."

I shall soon be laid at rest
  By my friends and comrades dear,
But the one that I love best
  She will not come nigh my bier.
Yet with my last parting breath,
  When cold, benumbed and chill,
I shall speak her name in death
  And behold her smiling still.

JEAN McINTYRE.

Aft, aft ha'e I wandered by Alva's green braes,
Aft there to my lass I ha'e sung sangs o' praise,
Aft wandered wi' her I did sae much admire,
My ain dawtie dearie, braw Jean McIntyre.

In spring when ilk wee bird was biggin' its nest,
I ha'e sported wi' her I lo'ed dearest and best,
'Twas then her dear charms set my bosom on fire
As I gazed on the beauty o' Jean McIntyre.

When simmer had come wi' the fu' blawn flowers
That were nursed into life by the saft April showers,
Of sweet converse with her I never did tire,
She was sae interestin', braw Jean McIntyre.

In the lang winter night by her auld faither's ingle,
Wi' lads and wi' lassies I aften did mingle ;
Hoo swiftly the hours sped while I did aspire
To win the pure heart o' braw Jean McIntyre.

SONG.

Come a' ye folk that lo'e a sang,
    And pass the hours alang wi' me,
The night before us yet is lang,
    Let's spend it then wi' mirth and glees.

    CHORUS:
    Noo let us a' sae happy be
        And spend the night with mirth and glee,
    Cement oor friendship wi' a sang
        And crack o' joys that winna dee,

We meet this night to honor him
    Wha amang the Poets stands sae hie
And wha was neither prood nor prim
    But liked wi' canty chiels to be.

CHORUS:

And he that 'mang us winna drink
    To the memory o' cor bardie slee,
May he e'er stand on poortith's brink
    And by his friends forgotten be.

CHORUS:

Awa ye gruesome sour-faced thrang,
    This warld's joys wha fear and dree,
Let me suggest ye're maybe wrang,
    Wha refuse wi' us to happy be?

CHORUS:

Here's to the land we lo'e sae dear,
    May blessings fa' frae heaven sae hie
Upon her sons baith far and near,
    And may they aye in friendship 'gree.

CHORUS:

CURLING SONG.

The winter is comin' wi' snaw and ice
And curling I hope will then be nice,
Then awa' wi' glee we will gae in a trice
To play a game on the ice, the ice.

CHORUS :
 We'll awa' to the ice, awa', awa',
 Though the ground be covered wi' snaw, wi' snaw,
 Though Boreas cauld does blaw, does blaw,
 We'll awa' to the ice, awa', awa'.

Then brithers a' let us stir aboot
And no be sweet though its cauld to gae oot,
The ice will be guid I ha'e nae doot,
And we'll play haud and haud aboot, aboot.

    CHORUS :
Noo awa we will gaug wi' mirth and glee,
And be as happy as bodies can be,
'Twill mak' oor hearts licht and young and frce
To curl oor staues up close to the tee.

On the ice we will curl wi' a' oor micht,
While every e'en shines clear and bricht ;
Soop it up will cry haud noo thats richt,
We'll put oor opoueuts in au unco plicht.

LIFE A FRAGMENT.

 Life in youth is like a bubbling fouutain
 Gushing from the bosom of the mountain,
 Meandering merrily on in its pride
 Happily, joyously down the hillside ;
 Rippliu.g o'er pebbles with musical clink,
 Kissing the wild flowers that grow on its brink,
 Glisteniug and sparkling ever and ever,
 Wending its way to the rolling river.

CAMPAIGN SONG NO. 1.

Our chosen clansmen tricd and brave,
    Have met with bonnet, plume and feather,
Like yoemen bold, in days of old,
    Their counsel wise to hold together,
And choose the man to lead the van
    Of loyal men from main to main,
So quick and short they doue the work.
    And made our chieftaiu James G. Blaine.

CHORUS :
Then hurrah ! hurrah ! now on we'll go
　Forth into battle once again ;
And with brave hearts we'll meet the foe,
　Led by our chieftain, James G. Blaine.

Another, too, shall lead us on,
　Who nobly fought our land to save ;
Whoe'er was known to stand his own,
　Aye, found the foremost of the brave.
Now let us make the welkin ring,
　With shouts at war-note of the slogan,
And quickly now fall into line
　At the command of John A. Logan.

CHORUS :
Then hurrah ! hurrah ! now on we'll go,
　While through this land is heard the slogan,
And bravely fight like freemen true,
　Led on this time by Blaine and Logan.

Now let us thank our comrades true
　For their deliberate, wise selection,
And with our votes their wisdom prove
　On next November at election
Then let us work with might and main,
　While through the land we hear the slogan,
Assured our work shall not be vain,
　With this our watch-word—Blaine and Logan.

CHORUS :
Then hurrah ! hurrah ! now on we'll go,
　When through the land is heard the slogan
And bravely gain, as freemen should,
　The victory under Blaine and Logan.

CAMPAIGN SONG NO. 2.
TUNE, "Scotland Forever."

Let the Democrats exult with joy o'er their selection,
   And on the wings of faith with hope triumphant rise.
And flatter their proud hearts that at the next election
   They shall seize with one more bound the long expected
     prize.
When they with joy supreme shall see their fondly
   cherished dream
At the last all fulfilled, and its rich fruition yield, ·
This their hope, long far-away desired now for many a
   day,
   O, at last to hold the sway, at last to win the field.
When the chiefs of their clans in counsel assembled,
   The sound of our war cry made their hearts to quake;
The boldest among them with fear and dismay trembled,
   The bravest among them did falter and shake;
O where shall we find a man bold enough to lead the van
   Forth into the conflict this time to succeed?
So throughout all the land, resolving again to stand,
   They chose Grover Cleveland their forces to lead.
Yet with courage undismayed, life's pulses they are
   bounding,
We would enter the arena, would engage in the fray,
And like valiant soldiers while the bugle blast is sounding,
   Would bear the palm of victory from the foe-man away.
Hear now that warlike strain, see the plumed knight of
   Maine,
   Foremost in the battle, in the thickest of the fight,
With loyal brave Logan nigh, shouting "On to victory,
   Now let us do or die, and God defend the right."

CAMPAIGN SONG NO. 3.
TUNE, "Battle Cry of Freedom."

Let us rally 'round our standard, boys, rally once again,
  Shouting the cry of right and freedom,
And march forth once more to the same old stirring
    strain,
  Shouting the cry of right and freedom.

CHORUS :
  Our party forever, hurrah, boys, hurrah,
  Down with the false men and up with the true,
  While we rally 'round our candidates, rally once again,
  Shouting the cry of right and freedom.

Let us rally 'round our leaders, the tried and the brave,
  Shouting the cry of right and freedom,
And never crouch to tyrants to be a willing slave,
  Shouting the cry of right and freedom.

Let us now add to our ranks a million voters more,
  Shouting the cry of right and freedom,
And fall into the line stretching out from shore to shore,
  Shouting the cry of right and freedom.

We will follow Blaine and Logan, once more to victory,
  Shouting the cry of right and freedom,
And on our opponents' faces defeat and shame we'll see,
  Shouting the cry of right and freedom.

CAMPAIGN SONG NO. 4.
TUNE, "Kingdom Coming."

Say, comrades, have you heard the good news
  That has come around this way?
The Democrats have nominated Grover Cleveland,
  Who they think will win the day.
A man who has done nothing at all
  To recommend his name ;
But I think about November, this fall,
  Will end his short-lived fame.

CHORUS :
He will stay at home, ha ! ha !
  We'll elect Jim Blaine, ho ! ho !
We know this result is surely coming,
  And we'll work to have it so.

Independents, too, have taken him up,
  And think they are very wise ;
They, too, shall drink the dregs of the cup
  And meet a great surprise.
The American people know too well
  Which of the two to trust,
And next November their minds will tell
  Like a jury wise and just.

CHORUS :
Now let each put his shoulder to the wheel
  And roll the car of progress on,
Of the fairest nation in all the world,
  On which the sun e'er shone.
Let each do his best and work with zeal
  To elect the man from Maine,
And our brave soldier boy from Illinois ;
  Leave Cleveland in the rain.

CHORUS :

CAMPAIGN SONG NO. 5.
Walk Around.

Who is the Democratic Presidential nominee ?
  One Stephen Grover Cleveland.
What service e'er was rendered to his native countrie
  By Stephen Grover Cleveland ?
He once was made the sheriff of Erie county.
  This Stephen Grover Cleveland ;
And served the county well in that capacity,
  Did Stephen Grover Cleveland ;
Afterwards he was elected Mayor of Buffalo,
  This Stephen Grover Cleveland ;

And while there he did nothing much to show
    For Stephen Grover Cleveland ;
And lastly he was made the Governor of New York,
    This Stephen Grover Cleveland ;
And as such has done some very dirty work,
    Poor Stephen Grover Cleveland.
Now this is all the reccomend his party have to show
    For Stephen Grover Cleveland ;
If there is anything more we have it yet to know
    About Stephen Grover Cleveland.

CAMPAIGN SONG NO. 6.

TUNE, "Scots Wha Hae."

Republicans, from shore to shore,
Awake, arise, go forth once more
To work with might the country o'er
    And gain the victory.
See, the foe confronts again,
Our army upon every plain,
Assured they will the battle gain,
    And shout with ecstacy.

Our leaders call us to the field,
Armed with buckler, sword and shield,
Determined ne'er to foe to yield,
    We follow bravely on.
By all the ties that we hold dear,
Like men we now should know no fear.
But firm and earnest and sincere
    We'll cross the rubicon.

While far and near, above, below,
Appears the cohorts of the foe,
With eager speed now on we go
    To show forth all our might ;
See, see athwart the autumn sky,
The banners of our foemen fly,
Now let us raise our loud war cry,
    And battle for the right.

CAMPAIGN SONG NO. 7.

TUNE, "Tramp, Tramp, the Boys are Marching."

For the next three mouths to come,
Amidst the tumult and the din,
Which will ensue throughout the land and nation,
Where each one will do his part
That his candidate may win,
However high or low may be his station.

CHORUS:
Tramp, tramp, tramp, the hosts are marching,
Through this great land of the free,
While beneath the starry flag we walk forth as before,
Let us ever live in peace and unity.

May we each consider well
The fitness of the men
Whom we would entrust with these great positions.
And in our mind of minds,
Ponder o'er and o'er again.
Which ones ere fitted best by our traditions.

CHORUS:

CAMPAIGN SONG NO. 8.

TUNE, "Star Spangled Banner."

O, say, have you seen, at the close of the day,
That bright star in the east now arising to glory,
Which long has been scattering bright ray after ray?
On, on, as we read in the pages of story.
See now it takes its stand, refulgent and grand,
Close to high zenith to smile on our land;
'Tis the bright star of far Maine, O, long may it shine
On this country of ours under favor divine.

In the heavens clearly seen this orb nightly appears,
On its way to the west, its light softly is beaming,
Its rays through the sky far above its compeers,
Wtth radiance and beauty the pathway is streaming.

Now behold its clear beam shining out from the stream,
Which reflects all its beauty more brightly, we deem,
'Tis the bright star of far Maine, O, long may it shine,
On this country of ours under favor divine.

O, now let us walk by the light of its ray,
  In the path of the just, as a people and nation,
And drive the last vestige of slavery away,
  And polygamy too which deserves condemnation.
Let us walk in the right and dare to do right,
And away from the darkness of error's black night,
While this bright star of far Maine still continues to shine
On this country of ours under favor divine.

CAMPAIGN SONG NO. 9.

I hear a song, oft borne along
  Upon the breeze now ev'ry day ;
From up far north it oft comes forth,
  To me a merry roundelay ;
But from the west it sounds the best,
  When westling winds bear on the strain ;
It sounds aloft—now loud, now soft—
  Elect our gallant son from Maine.

CHORUS :
Then sing the song, its notes prolong,
  So that the east may hear the strain,
So sweet, so fair, borne on the air,
  Elect ! elect our son from Maine.

The sunny South, from mouth to mouth,
  Trills it to many a merry tune,
So loud and clear, it strikes my ear,
  Borne on the balmy breeze of June.
Now like a feast the brave old east
  Takes up the stirring, glad refrain,
And says with zest, we'll do our best
  To elect our gallant son from Maine.

CHORUS :
Then sing the song, its notes prolong,
　Now while far East takes up the strain,
Now loud and clear, it strikes my ear,
　Elect ! elect our son from Maine.

CAMPAIGN SONGS, 1888.

Fellow Citizens, arise,
Noble countrymen, be wise,
And while time so swiftly flies
For Harrison and and Morton work ;
　Urge their claims throughout the land,
　Plead their cause from strand to strand.
　Nobly an unbroken band
For Harrison and Morton work.

CHORUS :
　For Harrison and Morton work,
　For Harrison and Morton work—
　Shout this refrain o'er the land,
　For Harrison and Morton work·

Soon we shall begin the fray,
Let us recruit then while we may,
Till the great eventful day,
For Harrison and Morton fight.
　Up now all brave boys in blue,
　Forward sons of veterans too,
　To the good old cause be true,
For Harrison and Morton fight.

Like chivalric knights of old
Our leaders are both true and bold,
Tried like pure refined gold ;
For Harrison and Morton vote.
　Swear then each true man and member,
　To work and fight and e'er remember
　On the sixth of next November,
For Harrison and Morton vote.

SONG 2.

The Democrats feel safely now,
While they at Baal's shrine do bow,
And their hearts with joy o'erflow
    From 'Frisco to Savannah.
So devoid of doubt or fear,
And rejoicing far and near,
They rend the air with cheer on cheer
    And wave the red bandana.

Their leader may be all they claim,
To them his be a glorious name,
And they may shout aloud his fame,
    One mighty to deliver;
But we have matched him by a man
Who ever marched in freedom's van,
Whose life his enemies may scan,
    A Roland for an Oliver.

Let them rejoice then while they may,
And glory that they now hold sway,
E'en boasting they will win the day
    They swear by Santa Anna;
But we shall meet them in the field,
Armed with justice as a shield,
Led by a man who ne'er shall yield.
    The man from Indiana.

So trusting in the sacred right,
We fear no foe, though great his might.
Once more again we now unite
    Our forces for the fray;
Side by side now on we go,
To hurl ourselves upon the foe,
And by one bold decisive blow
    To bear the prize away.

CAMPAIGN SONG.

Ben Harrison, my Jo Ben,
  When ye manhood's life began,
Ye early did resolve, Ben,
  To prove a worthy man,
And so you studied hard, Ben,
  As through college you did go,
And won distinction in your class,
  Ben Harrison, my Jo.

Ben Harrison, my Jo Ben,
  When first I came to know
The great worth of your character
  My heart was made to glow;
Affection's spark had kindled there,
  Fate's winds on it did blow,
Till brightly burned the sacred fire,
  Ben Harrison, my Jo.

Ben Harrison, my husband Ben,
  Through all the years that's sped,
Since by the sacred altar, Ben,
  Where you and I were wed,
I've often blessed the day, Ben,
  I've happy been I know,
As your devoted, loving wife,
  Ben Harrison, my Joe.

Ben Harrison, my Jo Ben,
  Being ever true and just
In all the work you've done, Ben,
  You' won the people's trust,
And they have you repaid, Ben,
  By honors high and so
Deserve your heart-felt gratitude,
  Ben Harrison, my Jo.

And now at last, my Jo Ben,
  They would confide to you
The highest place in all the land
  Because they know you true;

Though you may not command success,
  You can do more I know,
You can deserve it by your deeds,
  Ben Harrison, my Jo.

AN ANSWER TO A PIECE TAKEN FROM THE NEW YORK SUN AUGUST 13, 1888.

What's this I see and hear the noo,
  What's this I hear and see ?
Some man that surely has been fou
  Wi' a wee drap in his e'en,
Wi' a wee drap in his e'en nae doot,
  As blind as bat can be,
Some sheer nonsense has drivelled oot
  Aboot the G. O. P.

But let him rail wi' a his wit,
  Wi' his wit let him rail,
He'll find he has na clear coorse
  Wi' Cleveland's bark to sail :
Wi' Cleveland's bark to sail, my freends,
  He hes a stormy sea
Wi' billows high and tempests loud
  To daunt his heart o' glee.

He had to speak o' Harrison,
  Of him he had to speak,
In words baith light and flippant too,
  Yet a' sae very weak ;
Yet a' sae very week indeed,
  They weaker couldna be,
And fa' a' dunted to the grund
  When they strike sic as he.

At Jamie Blaine he had a fling,
  At him a fling he had,
His wit exhausted on the wing
  Draps doon and sinks to dee.

Draps doon ond sinks to dee in fear,
  As he comes hame again,
He dreads him like a Banqueo's ghaist,
  That chiel ca'd Blaine frae Maine,

What though he tries prophetic lear,
  Though prophetic lear he tries,
Cauld comfort he will get frae that,
  Drawn frae his barley bree.
Young Lochinavr o' a the west,
  Shall come sae bauld and slee
And seize his willin' laffin' bride
  Afore the haill countrie.

And then awa' wi' micht and main,
  Wi' micht and main rides he,
Till comin' to the grand white hoose
  Wi' muckle mirth and glee,
He there sits doon his bonnie bride
  In spite o' a' his faes,
While the Sun's bit prophet and his freens,
  Lament them ower their waes.

www.ingramcontent.com/pod-product-compliance
Lightning Source LLC
Chambersburg PA
CBHW030011030726
47499CB00008B/2995